Rosetta's
MAGICAL
READING JOURNEY

Rosetta's
MAGICAL
READING JOURNEY

LITTLE, BROWN AND COMPANY

New York ⚜ Boston

Little, Brown and Company

Hachette Book Group

1290 Avenue of the Americas, New York, NY 10104

Visit us at lb-kids.com

Little, Brown and Company is a division of Hachette Book Group, Inc.

The Little, Brown name and logo are trademarks of Hachette Book Group, Inc.

The publisher is not responsible for websites (or their content) that are not owned by the publisher.

First Edition: October 2016

Rosetta's Daring Day originally published in June 2007 by Disney Publishing Worldwide. *Rosetta's Dress Mess* originally published in February 2012 by Disney Publishing Worldwide.

Library of Congress Control Number: 2016936596

ISBN 978-0-316-31170-0

10 9 8 7 6 5 4 3 2 1

LSC-C

Printed in the United States of America

Rosetta's

MAGICAL
READING JOURNEY

Rosetta's Dress Mess

Written by
Laura Driscoll

Chapter 1

"Coming through!" Rosetta called. "Watch your wings!" The pretty red-haired garden-talent fairy raced down a fourth-floor hallway of the Home Tree. Fairies and sparrow men dove aside as she rocketed past.

"Rosetta!" a fairy called out to her. "I love your shoes! Is that the new style?"

"Yes!" Rosetta called back. "You should get a pair!" Then she raced on.

"Oh, Rosetta, wait up!" another fairy called to her. Rosetta slowed slightly. "Do these sleeves look better puffed out?" Melina asked. "Or pulled down?" She modeled the two options.

Rosetta took a moment to consider. "Puffed out," she decided. "But with that gorgeous hat, no one will be looking at your sleeves."

Melina beamed. A compliment from the best-dressed fairy in Pixie Hollow was enough to make any fairy's day!

Rosetta sped around a corner and down another hallway. At the very end of the hall, she landed, at last, in front of a door.

Rosetta's fairy glow flared with excitement as she rang the doorbell. Hem, a sewing-talent fairy, had made an announcement at breakfast in the tearoom. The sewing talents' next fashion show was going to take place in two days, just after sunset. Rosetta was determined to get a front-row seat.

You see, even though Rosetta was a garden-talent fairy, she loved clothes almost as much as she loved flowers!

Hem opened the workshop door. "Rosetta, you look fantastic! Come in!" she cried. "You're not the only garden talent in the workshop today." She opened the door wider. Lily stood by one of the tables.

"I lost a button," Lily said. A sewing talent named Serena was stitching a new one onto Lily's tunic.

Rosetta gave Lily a quick wave, then turned back to Hem. "So, Hem, I was just..." Rosetta's voice trailed off. What was that sparkly cloth in the corner? Her eyes darted around the room. Bolts of spider silk, linen, Queen Anne's lace, and thistledown lined one wall. Bins brimmed with flowers, sorted by color and size.

A dozen tables were set up around the workshop. By each table stood a figure made from straw. The sewing talents fitted their designs on these forms. The straw forms came in all sizes—from that of the smallest fairy in Pixie Hollow to the tallest. That way, the sewing talents could make each outfit perfect.

Rosetta sighed, taking it all in. This was one of her favorite places in the Home Tree.

"Rosetta?" Hem said. "You were saying?"

"Oh!" Rosetta snapped out of it. "I was just wondering if I could take a teensy-weensy peek at the new dresses?"

"Oh, all right," Hem said after a moment's

consideration. "But don't go telling every fairy what they look like. The surprise is part of the fun!"

Rosetta promised. Then she was off, flying around the workshop.

She stopped in front of a lacy fern dress. Tack was sewing on tiny green sea-glass beads. "What beautiful beads!" Rosetta cried. Tack's fairy glow flared with pride.

Then Rosetta noticed a small pile of clear beads on the table. "Wouldn't these clear ones reflect more light?"

Tack glared at Rosetta. "I like the green," he said.

Moving on to Taylor's worktable, Rosetta gasped. She ran her hand across the crinkly full skirt of Taylor's corn-husk dress. "How many layers does this have?"

"Four so far," Taylor said proudly. "Two more to go!"

"Looks fun to twirl in!" Rosetta said. "But..."

Taylor's brow wrinkled. "But what?" she asked.

"Well," Rosetta went on, *"I'd* add a crinkly sleeve to match the crinkly skirt!"

Taylor crossed her arms and gave a soft *harrumph.*

Across the room, Lily overheard Rosetta's words and bit her lip. "I think Rosetta means that the crinkliness is so beautiful...uh...she can't get enough of it! Right, Rosetta?"

But Rosetta was already flying off toward the next table. *Designing dresses is fun!* Rosetta thought. *I'm really good at this!*

Serena, now done with Lily's button, was pinning a sash onto her design. "That is such a pretty bathrobe!" Rosetta told her. "But where is your dress for the show?"

Serena ripped the sash off the dress and tossed it over her shoulder. "This *is* my dress for the show!" she said through gritted teeth.

Rosetta's fairy glow blushed. "Oh!" she said. "Silly me." She paused, trying to come up with a compliment. "It looks comfortable!" Then she hurried away.

Rosetta stopped to study every dress. She had a suggestion for each one. Niko, a sparrow man, was hemming a gardenia gown. "Poufier!" Rosetta cried.

"Needs more bows!" she told another fairy. "It's all about bows!"

Soon Rosetta had seen all the dresses.

She looked around the room. On her face was a huge smile.

But none of the sewing talents smiled back. In fact, they all looked...annoyed.

"What's the matter?" Rosetta asked.

Hem gently steered Rosetta toward the door. Lily followed. "It's nothing," Hem said. "We've just got a lot to do before the show!"

"Oh," said Rosetta. "Okay. But this was fun! Can I come back tomorrow?"

Hem thought for a moment. "I have a better idea," she said. "You have a lot of opinions. Very strong opinions! How would you like to design your *own* dress for the fashion show?"

Rosetta froze. Slowly, her eyes widened. Her wings started to beat a mile a minute. But she didn't make a sound, until—

"Eeeeeeeeeeeeeeee!" Rosetta squealed loudly.

When Rosetta took a breath, Lily rushed over and grabbed her hand. She pulled Rosetta away, out the door, and down the hall.

Over her shoulder, Lily called back to Hem. "I'm pretty sure that was a yes!"

Chapter 2

❀❀❀

Rosetta's head was still spinning as she and Lily flew outside into the Home Tree courtyard.

"Oh, my . . . I can't believe I get to design my own dress for the show!" she exclaimed. "Two days! That's not a lot of time."

"Not a lot of time for what?" came a voice nearby. Silvermist, a water-talent fairy, peeked out from under an umbrella plant.

"Oh, Silvermist!" Rosetta cried. "Listen to this. The sewing talents asked me to design a dress for the fashion show! Can you believe it?"

"Babbling brooks!" cried Silvermist. "That's fantastic, Rosetta!"

"I know," Rosetta went on. "I was giving them advice on their latest dresses. I guess they really loved my ideas."

Next to Rosetta, Lily cleared her throat. "That's not *exactly* how it went," she said.

Rosetta frowned. Then her face brightened. "Oh! You're right. I left out the part where Hem said I'm a very strong designer."

Lily put a hand on Rosetta's shoulder. "No, Rosetta," she said gently, "Hem said you have very strong *opinions*. And I'm not sure she meant it in a good way. I think you might have hurt their feelings."

"Hurt their feelings?" Rosetta repeated, shocked. "I just pointed out ways their dresses could be better." She shrugged. "That's helpful, not hurtful."

Lily nodded. "But how would you feel if a sewing talent came and suggested ways to make your garden prettier?"

Rosetta gave a half-snort. "Lily, that's different. *I* have a knack for designing dresses." *Really*, she thought. *A sewing talent who could improve on my garden? I'd like to see that!*

"I think Lily's right," Silvermist said. "If you told me you had a better way to gather dewdrops, I'd get teary-eyed."

At that moment, Fira, a light talent, flew up in a tizzy.

"Rosetta!" Fira cried. "You have to help me. All the light talents are having lunch with Queen Clarion tomorrow. And I have no idea what to wear!"

Rosetta's glow turned pink. "I'd be happy to help!" Then, with a quick wave to Lily and Silvermist, she zipped away with Fira.

Hurt feelings? Rosetta thought as she flew. She didn't think so. Maybe the sewing talents were...jealous? What if it turned out a garden fairy could design a better dress?

+ + +

Later, back in her room, Rosetta was ready to work on her dress design. She threw open the doors of her wardrobe. She looked through her dresses. She loved every single one of them. But she wanted to make something totally new.

She grabbed a feather pen from her writing desk. She jotted down a few quick notes.

First I need to pick the color, she thought. And where better to start than in one of the most colorful spots in Pixie Hollow? Her own garden!

When she got there, she flew past the roses. She had tons of rose dresses already. The same was true for daffodils, irises, tulips, daisies, lilies, honeysuckle, and pansies. Rosetta flitted all around the garden. Nope. Her dress material just wasn't here.

If not flower petals, then…leaves? Spider silk? Thistledown? No. It couldn't be anything that was on a shelf in the sewing workshop.

Rosetta heard rustling from the other side of some azaleas. She poked her head through the branches and gasped. Two hummingbirds were darting from flower to flower, sipping nectar.

As far as animals went, Rosetta didn't have a favorite. They were all either too dirty, too skittish, too loud, or too…wild. But Rosetta liked hummingbirds. They carried pollen from flower to flower, help- ing to make new ones. Best of all, they had the most beautiful feathers.

"*Hummingbird* feathers!" she cried and quickly wrote it down. "That's it!"

Rosetta had never, *ever* seen a dress made from shimmering hummingbird feathers. No wonder! Feathers of any kind were hard to come by. It would take forever to gather enough fallen feathers. It would be better to find a bird willing to give up some of his own. Luckily, Rosetta knew a certain animal talent who had a good hummingbird friend named Twitter. "I need to talk to Beck!" she decided.

Chapter 3

Rosetta headed straight for Beck's room. Near the Home Tree, she heard banging from the side of the old maple. Curious, she veered off course to check it out. She followed the curve of the great trunk around to the courtyard.

It was buzzing with activity. Dozens of fairies and sparrow men were hard at work. Woodworking fairies nailed twigs together, making a walkway. Painting fairies brushed on a coat of yellow mustard-seed paint.

Then Rosetta noticed Hem and some other sewing talents in the walkway's shadow.

Rosetta rushed over. "Hem! Is this—?"

"The runway for the fashion show!" Hem told her.

Rosetta gave a tiny squeal of excitement. She could picture it now. Every fairy's eyes on her dress. The shimmery feathers would catch the light of the firefly lanterns.

"Oh, Hem!" Rosetta called across the courtyard. "The runway needs to be longer. Fairies over here won't be able to see me—I mean, us." Rosetta flew over to Hem, who stood on the unfinished runway. "And don't you think there should be twice as many firefly lanterns?"

Hem waved over the woodworking fairies. They each carried a floorboard.

"Hem?" Rosetta moved in closer. "What do you think about a darker paint on the runway? A deep red would contrast with my dress so nicely. Hem? Hem?" She snapped her fingers in Hem's face.

Hem sighed. "Rosetta, please—"

Sandy, one of the woodworking fairies, turned around suddenly. She didn't know Rosetta had moved close behind her. *Thwap!* The floorboard on Sandy's shoulder whacked Rosetta right on the back of her head!

Flump! Rosetta dropped like a sack of acorns at the end of the runway.

"Knotty pines! Is she okay?" cried Sandy.

"Rosetta!" Hem gasped, kneeling at her side. "Rosetta? Can you hear me?"

Everyone breathed a sigh of relief when Rosetta opened her eyes. Hem, Sandy, and lots of sewing and woodworking talents stood over her.

"Oh, Rosetta!" Sandy moaned. "I'd fly backward if I could!

"Are you okay?" Hem asked.

Rosetta rubbed the back of her head. "What happened?" she asked.

"Take it easy," Hem said. "You were knocked out for a few wingbeats."

Rosetta stayed put for several minutes. Her ears were ringing and her head did feel a bit fuzzy. But slowly, it was all coming back to her.

She remembered the fashion show and the hummingbird-feather dress. She had been going to see Beck.

Rosetta brushed some sawdust from her

hair. When her knees stopped shaking, she rose into the air. With each minute, her wings felt stronger and her head felt less foggy. "I'm fine, really," she told Hem and Sandy.

"Are you sure?" Hem asked. "Maybe we should take you to the nursing talents?"

But Rosetta waved away Hem's concern. "I've got to go! I've got a dress to make!" As she flew off, Rosetta couldn't help adding, "It's going to be a showstopper!"

She was still rubbing her head as she landed in front of Beck's door. She knocked and heard Beck call, "Come in!"

"Beck, I need your help!" Rosetta blurted out. She quickly described her dress idea for the fashion show and her need for feathers. Then she stopped in the middle of a sentence. "Your hair looks great, by the way," she told Beck.

Beck stared at Rosetta. The stare became a squint. "Are you teasing me?" Beck asked. She tried to smooth her tangled hair. "I've been gathering chestnuts in the underbrush all day."

"No, I'm serious," said Rosetta.

"It's just that you never like my hair." She looked down at her simple leaf dress. "Or my clothes."

Huh, thought Rosetta. Now that she looked more closely, Beck's hair did look...messy. She rubbed her head. It still felt a little fuzzy. "So anyway," Rosetta said, getting back to her question, "could you ask Twitter if he could spare some feathers?"

Beck shook her head. "I can't do that. Twitter just molted. So did the other hummingbirds."

"Oh!" said Rosetta, disappointed. "Where are all the feathers they lost?"

Beck shrugged. "Who knows? Some here. Some there. Most get carried off by the wind, I guess."

Rosetta groaned. What a waste! All those gorgeous feathers. Dresses and dresses worth of feathers, gone! Then she had a brilliant idea. "I'll just take some of their *new* feathers!" she exclaimed.

"You don't understand, Rosetta," Beck explained. "The new ones take weeks to grow in fully. And plucking feathers hurts the birds."

Rosetta sighed. *Of all the times for birds to choose to molt!* she thought. *Right before a fashion show!*

No shimmery feathers. No dress. What would she do now?

Chapter 4

🌷🌷🌷

Rosetta had to think of another unique, showstopping dress design. But she wasn't worried. She was the best-dressed fairy in Pixie Hollow, so she was sure she'd come up with lots of good ideas. Her garden didn't have anything she wanted to use. But maybe someone else's did. Like Lily's!

Lily gave Rosetta a tour, pointing out

her most unusual flowers, but nothing jumped out at Rosetta.

"Maybe some strawberry blooms?" Lily asked. "They're very sweet."

Rosetta looked around Lily's tidy garden. Suddenly, a thought struck like a snapdragon snap. She was so caught up in the fashion show, she hadn't done a single thing in her own garden!

"Oh, sunflower seeds!" she exclaimed. "I haven't watered. I haven't weeded. What kind of garden fairy am I?"

Lily patted Rosetta's hand. "I knew you'd come arou—"

Rosetta cut her off. "I'm so glad you understand!" She flashed her sweetest smile. "So you'll keep an eye on my garden for me? Just until after the fashion show?"

Lily raised one eyebrow. "Me? Uh, sure, Rosetta. I'd be happy to."

Rosetta smiled. That was a relief. She knew her garden would be in excellent hands.

She moved on to Bess's art studio. She told Bess that she was making a dress for the fashion show. "I figure art fairies know about color and design," Rosetta said. "Maybe I'll be inspired by one of your paintings!"

Rosetta loved Bess's landscapes of Pixie Hollow. She loved her portraits of Queen Clarion. But she didn't get an idea for her design. As she turned to go, something on a hook by the door caught her eye.

She lifted the thin cotton garment off the hook. It had the most unusual pattern, with splotches of color here and there.

"How interesting! Bess, which sewing-talent fairy made this?"

Bess gave her an odd look. "Umm... that's an art smock."

Rosetta's glow went pink. "Oh, uh... of course! I knew that. But can I see it on you?"

Bess put the smock over her tunic and leggings. Rosetta grabbed a length of picture-hanging cord from a table. She tied the cord around Bess's waist like a belt. Then she steered Bess over to a mirror.

"Well?" Rosetta said. "What do you think?"

Bess hesitated. "I think... I think it looks like an art smock. With a picture-hanging cord for a belt."

Rosetta's shoulders drooped like a daisy in need of water. *She's right*, Rosetta thought.

I'm so desperate for a great idea, I'm letting it get to me!

By dinnertime, Rosetta felt completely lost. Designing a dress was harder than it looked. She only had tomorrow and part of the next day! If she didn't think of something soon, she wouldn't have time to make *any* dress.

She considered the tablecloths and the heavy drapes in the tearoom. *I could sew together floral-print cloth napkins*, she thought. *You wouldn't have to worry about spilling on it.* She shook her head, scrapping the idea.

Rosetta anxiously tapped her fingers on the table. There had to be an idea here! At that moment, a fairy floated past her. Wait! What was she wearing? The fairy's garment was simple, in a stiff, heavy fabric, with some kind of small bow in the back.

It was a full minute before Rosetta realized what she was looking at. The fairy was Dulcie, a baking talent. And she was wearing an apron. A plain kitchen apron.

Rosetta could not leave the tearoom quickly enough.

"What is wrong with me?" Rosetta wondered aloud as she made a beeline for her room. All she wanted was to sit quietly and think. First Bess's art smock, and now Dulcie's apron? A napkin dress? Rosetta had been making style missteps all day. And then there had been that moment at Beck's. Her messed-up hair had seemed stylish. Rosetta hadn't had one good fashion idea since.

She gasped and stopped in midair. "Since before I got hit on the head!" she cried. Before that, the good ideas had been coming fast and furious. Since then, nothing! It was as if the knock on the head had changed her. It was as if... she had *lost* her sense of style!

Chapter 5

That night, Rosetta slept terribly, and she woke up feeling as if she hadn't slept a wink. How was she supposed to come up with a wonderful dress design if she wasn't even well rested? Frustrated, she threw the pillow across the room. It knocked the lampshade off her firefly lamp.

She pushed off her thistledown blanket

and got up. "Today is a new day," she said. "Maybe I'm back to my old self."

But one look inside her wardrobe and her fears flooded back. She had no idea what to wear.

Rosetta's heart sank. The fashion show was the next day. She didn't have a dress. She didn't have a plan. And now she didn't really have a hope. If anything, she was more confused than yesterday.

Rosetta reached into her wardrobe. She grabbed a skirt and top and threw them on. Then she scooped a sun hat up off the floor. Even a fairy with no sense of style knows to protect her face from the sun. The last thing she needed was a sunburn.

A few minutes later, Rosetta flew slowly into the tearoom. It was still early for breakfast. Only a few other fairies were scattered around the room—mostly baking and serving talents. Then Rosetta noticed Tinker Bell at the pots-and-pans-talent table. Tink waved Rosetta over.

"Wow!" Tink cried. "That's some outfit!"

"Is it?" Rosetta asked, hope filling her voice.

Tink pointed to the hat on Rosetta's head. "Is that...a lampshade?"

Rosetta took it off and looked at it for the first time. "I guess it is," she said. She shrugged and put it back on her head. She was too worried to care.

"What are you doing up so early?" Tink asked her.

"I woke up and couldn't get back to sleep." Rosetta felt tears welling in her eyes. "My fashion sense got knocked out of me yesterday. I've probably lost it forever."

She dropped into the chair next to Tink. Putting her head down on the table, she let the tears spill out. In between sobs, she tried to explain.

"Fashion sense?" Tink said when Rosetta was done telling her story. "Who needs it? Now you probably have more *common* sense! Just look at me. I wear the same thing every day."

Rosetta did look at Tink. Then she put down her head again and wailed. The same thing? Every day? How tragic!

"*Shhh*, Rosetta," Tink said. "Quiet down. That's enough. Oh, all right, I'll help you, I'll help you! Just stop crying already."

"How can you help me?" Rosetta asked.

Tink's idea was simple. "A whack on the head knocked your fashion sense out of whack. So maybe another will whack it back into place!"

Rosetta wasn't sure this was a very good idea, but Tink sure seemed convinced it would work.

They found some extra floorboards under the runway. Tink took a few practice swings with one. "Hold still," Tink commanded. "On the count of three—"

"Wait!" Rosetta cried. "I'm not ready yet." This was crazy, but the truth was, she really, *really* wanted to design a dress for the show. The clock was ticking.

"Let's go," Rosetta said at last. She took a deep breath. "Not too hard," she said firmly. "And try not to mess up my hair." Then she turned her back on Tink. She closed her eyes and braced for the blow.

Tink wound up and—Rosetta ducked. The board sailed over her head, and Tink spun around in a full circle.

"No, don't!" Rosetta covered her head with her hand. She stayed like that for several long moments. Then she stood up straight and tall again. She closed her eyes. "Okay. I'm ready now."

"Are you sure?" Tink waited until Rosetta nodded. "Here goes. One . . . two . . . th—"

"*AAAH!*" Rosetta ducked again. "I can't help it! I just—it's really hard to—"

"Let someone hit you with a board?" Tink said. "I can't say that I blame you."

"*Oooooo!*" Rosetta stomped her foot. "But how can I let this idea go without even trying it? I'll never know if it would have worked!"

Tink lowered the floorboard. The two fairies sat down side by side on the runway.

Both were deep in thought.

Then Tink sat bolt upright. "Aha!" she said. "What if you don't *know* when I'm going to whack you on the head?"

"What?" said Rosetta.

"I could follow you around," Tink said, her eyes lighting up. "In secret!"

"You mean you'd sneak up on me? You'd do that?" Rosetta asked.

Tinker Bell shrugged. "What are friends for?"

Chapter 6

Rosetta and Tink agreed on three rules. First, Tink couldn't hit Rosetta too hard. Second, no sneaking up on her while she was sleeping. And third, Tink wasn't allowed to tell anyone about it.

"After all, I don't want everyone to know I've lost my style!" Rosetta said.

Rosetta and Tink shook hands on it. Then they flew off in different directions.

Rosetta headed for her garden. She had

two goals for the day. Make a dress. And keep busy! She couldn't sit around waiting for Tink to strike!

Rosetta had to admit, spending time with Tink had changed her attitude. Tink was a real go-getter. An hour ago, Rosetta had been ready to give up. But Tink had inspired her. "I'm going to find lots of pretty things," she vowed. "And I'm going to make them into a dress!" Her shoulders drooped slightly. "Somehow," she whispered.

As Rosetta neared her garden, her spirits lifted. She hadn't been there for a day and a half, and she missed it. She missed the sun on the daylilies and the dew-speckled violets. She missed the colors, smells, and sounds of her garden.

Rosetta took a deep breath as she entered the garden. Right away, her problems seemed smaller. She looked around. Her garden looked wonderful, as if she hadn't been gone at all. Just then, Lily's head popped up from behind a patch of buttercups.

"Oh!" cried Rosetta, startled. "Lily, you're here! The garden looks so lovely. You're so sweet to take care of it for me!"

"Rosetta!" said Lily. "I didn't recognize you at first in that . . . really interesting hat."

Rosetta put a hand to her head. *Oops!* She'd forgotten to take off the lampshade.

Another familiar face popped up next to Lily's.

"Silvermist!" Rosetta cried.

The water-talent fairy gave Rosetta a little wave. "I'm just helping out with the watering."

"That's so nice of you!" Rosetta said. She knew she should feel grateful. Lily and

Silvermist were doing her a huge favor. But she felt a pang of jealousy, too. *Nearly two days without me*, thought Rosetta. *And my flowers seem as happy as ever. Happier, even. It's as if they don't need me at all!*

"Are you done with the dress?" Silvermist asked. "I can't wait to see it."

Her question shook Rosetta back to her plan for the day. "Actually, I was about to head out," she said. She crossed her fingers behind her back. "To look for finishing touches."

"I'd love to come with you!" Silvermist exclaimed.

"Oh, yes!" said Lily. "Can we, Rosetta? It would be a treat to watch a genius at work!"

Rosetta hesitated. "Uh, you don't have to do that. You've both been so helpful already."

"But it would be fun!" Lily insisted.

Rosetta tried to talk them out of it. But in the end, she just couldn't say no.

With Lily and Silvermist following, Rosetta led the way. *Where to?* she wondered. The first thing that popped into her head was Havendish Stream. So she flew in that direction.

"So what are you looking for?" Lily asked.

"Oh, you know," Rosetta said. "A little of this. A little of that."

Silvermist chuckled. "I get it. Your design is top secret!"

If only! Rosetta thought. But if they thought she was being mysterious.... Well, maybe that could work. Rosetta hovered and looked around Havendish Stream.

She simply had to choose something here. But what? Directly below her was a moss-covered rock. "Aha!" she exclaimed, as if she had been looking for it all along. She tore off a large piece of the soft green plant. She rolled it up and tucked it under one arm.

Lily and Silvermist nodded. "Moss," said Lily. "Interesting."

They watched Rosetta fly this way and that. She wandered toward some reeds at the water's edge. She pulled three of them. Then she plucked a small heart-shaped lily pad from the stream. She handed the items to Silvermist. "Could you carry these?" she asked.

"Of course!" Silvermist replied. She looked at the hodgepodge of things in her hands. Jokingly, she suggested another item. "How about those waterlogged bits of wood rush over there?"

"Oh, yes! That might work, too," Rosetta

replied. *I can't imagine how*, she thought. *But I might be missing something. Maybe bringing along Silvermist and Lily was a good idea after all!*

At Rosetta's reply, Silvermist's merry expression clouded with confusion. She and Lily followed Rosetta away from the stream. They flew deeper into the woods. On the way, Rosetta picked up some drab toadstools. Silvermist winked at Lily and pointed to a piece of pine branch. "How about this?" she asked Rosetta.

"Um...sure!" Rosetta said.

"And this?" Silvermist tried. She held up a strange-looking seedpod.

Rosetta hesitated and looked it over. "Yes, let's take that."

Silvermist handed some of the items to

Lily for her to carry. "So, you...have plans for these things, Rosetta?"

"Uh, yes," Rosetta replied. But she didn't sound very sure of herself.

Flying through the dairy mouse pasture, Rosetta picked five cloverleaf stems. She left the pink clover flowers behind.

"Don't you want the flowers?" Lily asked her. "They're pretty..."

"Oh! Of course," said Rosetta, trying to cover. How could she, a garden talent, have overlooked the flowers!

Silvermist was eyeing Rosetta. As they headed back into the woods, Silvermist flew close beside her.

"Rosetta, are you feeling okay?" she asked. "You don't seem yourself."

Rosetta forced a laugh. "I'm fine. Just

fine." She felt a pang of guilt. Silvermist and Lily were being good friends to her, and she was fibbing to them.

Silvermist's eyes narrowed. "Really?" she asked. "If I didn't know better, I'd guess you have no idea what you're looking for."

Rosetta stared up at the sky, down at the ground—anywhere but at Silvermist. She opened her mouth to answer. She wasn't sure what words would come out.

Just then, in a flash, a blond-haired fairy in a short green leaf-dress zipped out from behind the oak tree. She swung a large stick at Rosetta's head.

"Rosetta, duck!" Silvermist yelled. The stick whistled over Rosetta's head, missing it by a hair.

"Tinker Bell!" Lily gasped. "What in Pixie Hollow are you doing?"

Chapter 7

Rosetta held up her hands to calm Silvermist and Lily. "It's okay! Tink's trying to help me."

"Help you?" Lily cried. "She just tried to bonk you on the head with a stick!"

Rosetta took a deep breath. "I know. It doesn't make sense. But it's the truth." Rosetta told them the whole story. She started with her hummingbird-feather-dress idea. She told them about the knock on the head at the runway and what had happened since then. And she told them about her talk with Tink and their plan to knock some fashion sense *back* into her.

Silvermist and Lily were quiet for a moment. Then Silvermist said, "Well, I guess that would explain your outfit, Rosetta." She turned to Tink. "But Tink, really?"

"It could work!" Tink insisted.

"And I want to give it a try," Rosetta added. "Something definitely happened when that floorboard hit me, and I just want to feel like my old self again."

Silvermist, Lily, and Tink flew to Rosetta's side. Silvermist wrapped an arm around her shoulder. "Aw, cheer up, Rosetta," Silvermist said. "We are, after all, just talking about *clothes—*"

"But I—" Rosetta interrupted.

"And I *know*," Silvermist went on, "that clothes are something you like a lot. So Rosetta, I'd like to introduce you to some fairies who can help you."

"Who?" Rosetta asked.

Silvermist flew between Tink and Lily. She put an arm around each of them. "Us!" she exclaimed.

Lily's face lit up. "Yes!" she said. "We'll help you make a dress."

Rosetta thought about it. Yesterday she would have said no. But a lot had changed since then. And Rosetta felt better now that her friends were around her.

She smiled a big smile. "Would you do that?"

"Of course!" Lily cried.

"Absolutely!" Silvermist agreed.

But Tink looked unsure. "Clothes? They're

not my thing," she said. "But…I'm in *if* I can keep my old job, too."

"What?" said Lily. "Do you mean hitting Rosetta on the head when she's not looking?"

Tink nodded and grinned.

"Deal," Rosetta said. *Maybe this can all work out*, she thought. *By the fashion show tomorrow, Tink will have bonked me on the head. I'll be all better, and I'll have a dress!*

With the toe of her slipper, Tink kicked at the moss. "Do you want to take this… stuff?" she asked Rosetta.

Rosetta took one look at the pile of brown toadstools, seedpods, and pine needles. "Leave it," she said. "I don't know what I was thinking."

The four fairies headed back toward the Home Tree.

"Here's the plan," Rosetta said when they reached the courtyard. "Let's split up. Grab some things we might be able to use. Then meet back in my room. I'll get us some dinner from the kitchen."

They all zipped off in different directions. Rosetta headed for her room. In the lobby of the Home Tree, she passed a group of fairies. Three of them were wearing unusual hats.

Rosetta looked closer. Were they hats? Or...

Lampshades! Rosetta couldn't help giggling. *Well, that's something,* she thought. *I've lost my sense of style. But I'm still a trendsetter!*

Chapter 8

W hat's keeping Tinker Bell?" Rosetta
wondered. Outside, the moon was up.

She fluttered around her room as Lily
and Silvermist unpacked their finds. The
three of them had finished their cups of
pumpkin soup. But Tink's was getting cold.

A knock came at the door. "Oh, good!
That must be her!" Rosetta flew across the
room. She threw open the door. "Whoa!"
she cried, darting backward.

Stick in hand, Tink had taken a swing at her.

"Nice try, Tink," said Rosetta. "But I knew it was you."

Tink snapped her fingers. "So close!" She picked up a wooden crate next to the door and took it into Rosetta's room.

The fairies gathered at the foot of Rosetta's bed. "Okay," she said. "What have we got?"

Silvermist went first. She showed them a seaweed bag filled with blue sea-glass beads and bits of shiny shells. "This is my favorite part," she said, pulling out a deep-purple water lily blossom. "The dress could be long and flowing, with sea glass and shells for sparkle!"

Rosetta nodded. "Very…water fairy."

Silvermist laughed, then shrugged. "That's me!"

Lily went next. She held up an orange tiger lily blossom and several handfuls of pink phlox buds. She also had one perfectly shaped red tulip. "How about a tulip skirt, a phlox-bud top, and a tiger lily hat?"

Rosetta liked bright colors. But would it be too much? She didn't trust herself to know anymore.

"You're going to love what I brought," Tink said. She upended her crate with a loud *clatter, clatter, clunk*. Several pieces of copper lay in a heap with a hammer and what looked like a teapot handle.

"Oh, wait!" Tink cried, picking up the hammer. "That's not for the dress. That's for me." She jammed it into the tool belt she was wearing. "This dress needs some tinker touches. Something metallic!"

"So, Rosetta," said Silvermist, "how about you?"

"I had some ideas about a hat and shoes," Rosetta said. She held up a spiky purple thistle puff and some ladyslipper flowers from her garden. "As for the dress, I'm stumped."

"That's okay," said Lily. "Silvermist, Tink, and I have plenty of ideas."

Silvermist nodded. "Which did you like best?"

Rosetta thought about it. "Well...I... *hmm*..."

"Long and flowing would be very fancy," Silvermist pointed out.

"But a tulip dress would be playful," Lily said.

"No, no," said Tink. "We've all seen

dresses like those. But have any of you *ever* seen a copper dress?"

"No, and there's a good reason for that," Silvermist said with a chuckle.

Tink, Silvermist, and Lily turned back to Rosetta. She knew they were waiting for her decision. But she had no idea what to say.

Finally, she threw up her hands. "I don't know!" she cried. She flopped down onto her bed. "I just don't know. And we can't use them all."

The room was silent for a moment. Then Rosetta suddenly sat up. "Wait! Maybe we *can* use them all!"

"How?" asked Lily, sitting down next to Rosetta.

"What if we each make a part of the

dress?" Rosetta explained. "Then we'll put the pieces together and . . . *ta-da!*"

Lily nodded. "That just *might* work."

Silvermist agreed. "It would be different, anyway."

Tink offered Rosetta and Lily each a hand. They grabbed on, and Tink pulled them up off the bed. "Sounds good to me!" she said.

They agreed on a plan. Silvermist would make the skirt. Lily would make the top. Tink would handle the sleeves. And Rosetta would make the hat and slippers.

Each fairy picked a corner of Rosetta's room. They settled in and got right to work. For the better part of two hours, the room was quiet, except for random hammering from Tink's corner.

At one point, Rosetta noticed she hadn't heard Tink's hammering in a while. Then the quiet was broken by the whir of wings close behind her.

"I hear you, Tink," said Rosetta. She knew without looking up that Tink was trying to sneak up on her.

"So close!" Tink whispered. She dropped her stick and flew back to her corner.

Not long after that, the fairies gathered together once again. They took turns pinning their parts of the dress to a straw fairy form Rosetta kept next to her wardrobe.

Rosetta was the last. She placed the thistle-puff hat on the straw fairy's head. She set the ladyslipper slippers at its base. Then they all took a step back and studied the outfit.

Lily had pieced all three flowers—the

red tulip, the orange lily, and the pink phlox—in an eye-catching top. Meanwhile, Silvermist's skirt was loaded with sea glass and shells sewn in a swirl pattern. For the sleeves, Tink had lashed together copper bangles. Each piece of the dress was beautiful in its own way.

"It's definitely one of a kind!" Tink said finally.

"Yes," Lily agreed. "That is really something."

"Something...unusual," Silvermist said.

"Weeping willows!" Rosetta exclaimed. "That is *awful*."

Chapter 9

The next morning, Rosetta rolled over in bed and opened her eyes. She squinted at the crazy mess of a dress hanging on the door of her wardrobe. She laughed just looking at it. The night before, all four fairies had had a good laugh, too—after the disappointment had worn off.

Rosetta sighed and got out of bed. They had given it a try, and that was that. Today at sunset, the sewing talents would put on the fashion show. But Rosetta wouldn't have a dress in it. What would the sewing fairies think? Her glow turned pink with embarrassment.

Face it! thought Rosetta. *I'm not a sewing talent. I'm a garden-talent fairy.* She froze. The thought wasn't meant to be comforting, but it was, somehow. "I'm a garden fairy!" she repeated out loud.

She raced to her wardrobe. She threw on a dress and a wide-brimmed straw hat. She slipped her feet into her gardening boots.

Rosetta flew downstairs and right through the tearoom—in one door and out the open window. When she came out, she had a warm poppy puff roll in each hand.

Soon she was at her favorite breakfast spot in her garden. She settled onto the patch of velvety moss under a large sword fern.

"*Ahhh,*" she sighed. "Home, sweet home." She nibbled on a roll while the song of a nearby warbler danced in her ears. *I haven't been this relaxed in days,* she thought. After she ate, Rosetta got busy. Lily had taken very good care of everything, but there was still plenty to do. She spent the early morning watering. Then she weeded through late morning. Not until late afternoon did Rosetta take a break. "Sweet sunflower seeds!" she exclaimed, noticing the long shadows. She had lost all sense of time. When her stomach rumbled, she realized it was almost dinnertime. But she wasn't ready to leave her garden just yet.

Feeling worn out, she hopped up onto a toadstool. She closed her eyes and lay back, her spine curving along the toadstool's top. Her feet and her head hung down over the sides. When she opened her eyes, her garden looked different. It took a wingbeat for her to realize she was seeing it upside down.

At that very moment, a beam of late-afternoon sunlight pierced the trees. The orange light shone through the petal of a peach-colored rose. The petal glowed with fiery warmth. Rosetta gasped. She had never seen such an intense color before. At the same time, the light hit several droplets of water trapped at the base of the petal. The light split into tiny rainbows, stretching between the flower and the ground below.

It was so beautiful, it took Rosetta's breath away.

And to think I sit on this toadstool nearly every day, she said to herself. *I look at my garden from this spot all the time! But never like this.*

Rosetta felt as if she were seeing her garden for the first time. A wave of pride swelled in her. She had created this wonderful place. She had planted it and tended it, day after day. And now one ray of light had reopened her eyes to its beauty.

Too soon, the moment was gone. The light shifted and the rainbows vanished. The peach rose lost its glow. Rosetta lay there a second longer. The rose was tilting back. Wait! It wasn't the rose. It was her. She felt herself slipping, falling. *Bonk!*

She tumbled in a heap to the ground. But a second later, she bounced back up. She was refreshed, revived, and more energetic than she had been all day. But was it more than just energy? She felt inspired! It was as if there were nothing she couldn't do. *Oh! Why couldn't I have felt this way yesterday? Or the day before? That's when I really needed it.*

She had a funny idea and couldn't help laughing out loud. "Now, if only I had looked at our *crazy dress* upside down..." The words nearly bowled her over like a herd of runaway sprinting thistles. She had an idea. She had a great, clever, original idea.

Just then, she heard voices. They were coming from the climbing-rose arch. *"Ro-set-taaaa!"* someone was calling.

Speeding over, Rosetta saw Lily and Silvermist flying toward her. "Oh! There you are!" Lily said. A look of concern clouded her face. "How are you?"

"We were worried," said Silvermist. "We haven't seen you all day. And after last night—*whoa!*"

Without stopping, Rosetta grabbed them

both by the hand. She pulled them along behind her. "The fashion show!" she shouted over her shoulder. "We don't have much time! We have to finish our dress!"

Silvermist and Lily looked completely confused.

"What?" Lily asked.

"The dress is a mess," Silvermist said gently. "Don't you remember?"

Rosetta laughed but didn't say another word until they were back in her room.

"This dress *is* a mess...but maybe it's closer to perfect than we thought!"

While Lily and Silvermist watched, Rosetta went to work. She snipped the stitches that held the pieces of the dress together. Then, taking the pieces, she ducked behind a changing screen.

Lily and Silvermist waited patiently.

They heard more snipping. They heard rustling fabric. When they heard hammering, they started to worry.

"Is everything okay?" called Lily.

"Just...about done...," Rosetta called. "Are you ready?" She flew out from behind the screen. She was wearing a completely different dress. Or was she?

Lily and Silvermist looked closely and saw the pieces they had made. But Lily's colorful top was now the skirt. Silvermist's flowing skirt was now the top. As for Tink's sleeves, Rosetta had taken them apart. She'd linked the copper bangles together into a funky necklace.

"I turned our dress upside down!" Rosetta explained.

"Stormy seas, that's *so* much better!" Silvermist exclaimed.

"It's great!" Lily said. "How in Pixie Hollow did you think of doing that?"

Rosetta smiled and shrugged. "I just got inspired," she said. "Do you think it's good enough for the fashion show?" Even as she asked, she knew the answer.

She didn't doubt herself anymore. It was a beautiful dress, and her fashion sense was back. Still, it made her feel good when both Lily and Silvermist cried, "Yes!"

"But we have to hurry," added Lily, peeking out the window. "The sun! It's almost to the horizon!"

Rosetta zipped to the door. She threw it open and led the way through.

Thwap! A stick swung out into the doorway. It struck Rosetta on the forehead.

Flump! Rosetta dropped like a sack of acorns onto the floor.

Chapter 10

Rosetta's eyes fluttered open again before Silvermist and Lily had finished scolding Tinker Bell.

"She didn't need to be thumped. She was already better!" Lily was saying.

Rosetta waved a hand. "It's okay," she said. "I'm okay. Really." She tried to sit up.

"Wait. Don't rush it," said Silvermist.

But Rosetta insisted. "I have to rush it. Or we'll miss the show!"

"I know!" said Tink. "Let's test her. Rosetta, what do you think of my dress?"

"Well..." Rosetta hesitated for a moment. "I would say...make the skirt longer. Add sleeves. And more color. Or maybe it would be easier to start from scratch?"

Lily, Silvermist, and Tink burst out laughing. "That sounds like the Rosetta we know!" Lily said.

"See?" said Tink. "My plan worked perfectly!"

Now Rosetta laughed, too. "What was I thinking?" she said. "I can't believe I went along with your crazy plan! But we'll talk about that later. Let's get this dress to the fashion show!"

Rosetta jumped to her feet and led the way, racing down the hall. They reached the central stairwell and darted downward. They could hear clapping and cheers from outside. The fashion show was under way!

Tink, Lily, and Silvermist went to find seats in the audience while Rosetta flew on, through the window, into the Home Tree courtyard. The crowd of fairies looked up as she raced overhead. She zipped toward the runway, then ducked backstage. Hem stood there, clipboard in hand.

"Hem!" Rosetta called in a loud whisper. "I'm here! Can I still go on?"

Hem smiled. "You're just in time, Rosetta!" she said. "And you look beautiful! Wait here! I'll announce you!"

Hem flew out onstage. Rosetta could hear her address the crowd. "We have a dress by a very special guest designer," Hem said. "She's a garden fairy with a passion for fashion. Everybody, give a big hand to...Rosetta!"

Two sewing fairies pulled the curtain flaps apart. And the next moments were a lot like Rosetta had imagined they would be. The crowd was clapping. Every fairy's eyes were on her. But Rosetta's eyes were on three smiling faces in the crowd: Tink, Lily, and Silvermist. They were clapping and cheering for Rosetta the loudest of all. Rosetta's glow flared brightly. But it wasn't because of pride or excitement. Rosetta was full of gratitude. She had the best friends any fairy could ask for.

Once offstage, she hurried around front and found a seat in the audience. The show wasn't over yet. There were still a few more dresses to see! Taylor flew out, modeling her corn-husk dress. Then came

Tack. Rosetta had to admit the green beads were perfect. Serena finished the show with a dress that was simple and flowing. It looked nothing like a bathrobe.

Now Rosetta was the one clapping and cheering loudest of all. There were so many pretty dresses! Maybe if she asked really, really nicely, Hem would let her borrow one. Or two. Or three.

Rosetta's Daring Day

Written by
Lisa Papademetriou

Chapter 1

"Rosetta! Come quick!" Fawn fluttered wildly into the garden.

Rosetta's head was deep inside a lily's bloom when she heard Fawn calling her. Rosetta was a garden-talent fairy and had been stirring up the pollen. She popped her head out. "What is it?"

When Fawn caught sight of her friend, she tried to stop. But she was going too fast. She crashed into a bright-red rose.

"My rose!" Rosetta cried. She flew past Fawn and over to the flower. Half its petals were gone. "Fawn, what are you doing?" she demanded.

"*Oops!*" Fawn started picking up the red petals. "It's just that we're about to start a game of acorn ball and I was wondering if you'd like to join us."

"Not really, Fawn," Rosetta said. Rosetta didn't care for games or sports. She liked beautiful things, such as flowers and frilly dresses and delicate petal shoes. "I've got a lot of work to do in the garden."

"What work?" Fawn gave Rosetta a doubtful look. "Everything looks perfect!"

Rosetta sighed. "You're such an animal talent," she said. "Anyone can see that the garden is a *disaster*!"

Rosetta didn't really think that her

garden was a mess. In fact, she thought it looked quite pretty. But Rosetta didn't want to play acorn ball. It meant flying here and there and tossing an acorn around and trying to tag other fairies. The last time she had played, her hair had gotten terribly tangled.

"A disaster?" Fawn repeated. "It looks beautiful to me."

Rosetta couldn't help a small, proud smile. "You think so?" Her glow turned as pink as her rose-petal dress. She cleared her throat. "Well, never mind. I've still got a lot of work to do."

"Maybe I could help you," Fawn suggested. "If we worked together, we would get done faster. Then you could play with us."

Rosetta flew to the end of the row of

daffodils, where a careless bunny had trampled a leaf. "If you really want to help me, tell the rabbits to stay out of my garden!" She propped up the leaf with a twig and sprinkled it with water.

Fawn smiled. "I can tell them, but I doubt they'll listen," she said. "Rabbits have big ears, but they also have minds of their own. They don't like getting bossed around. So, Rosetta, how about it—do you want me to help you pull some weeds?"

"You don't know the difference between a weed and a prize orchid!" Rosetta replied.

"That's true," Fawn said with a sigh. She was clearly disappointed. Rosetta felt a stab of guilt for hurting her friend's feelings.

"It's okay, Fawn," Rosetta said. "Working in the garden is my talent, just like working with animals is yours. Go ahead and play acorn ball. Then you can come back and tell me all about it. It will be like I was there."

Fawn grinned. "All right, I will!" She turned and zipped off toward the field near the Home Tree. "I'll be back soon!" she called over her shoulder.

Rosetta waved one of the rose petals like a leafkerchief at her friend. Then she flew to the morning glories to check the shady side of the garden.

In the shadow of a nearby maple tree was a green patch that Rosetta loved. It was always cool, even when the sun was hot. A special silvery fern grew there. It had just poked up from the earth and was curled into tight fists. They were called fiddle-heads at this stage. They could be cooked up in the kitchen into a crisp, delicious treat. But Rosetta wouldn't let anyone pick the fiddleheads. She loved them too much.

Rosetta perched atop a rock among the morning glories. "*Ahh,*" she said. "The garden is so quiet. So peaceful. So—"

A loud noise cut through the silent garden. It was a squirrel making quite a racket.

"Oh, be quiet!" Rosetta said to the squirrel. She could see him standing on a tree limb overhead. He swished his fluffy red tail.

"Can't you see that I'm trying to have a relaxing moment in my garden?" Rosetta shouted. But the squirrel didn't give up. He ran along the limb, back and forth, chattering nonstop. Rosetta plugged her ears. It didn't help.

"You can quit trying to talk to me. I'm

not an animal talent," Rosetta told the squirrel. "I can't understand a word you're saying, and I wouldn't care even if I could."

She let out a frustrated sigh as the squirrel's chatter got even more frantic. "That's it. This squirrel is driving me nuts!" There was only one solution. She'd have to go find Fawn. Maybe an animal talent could convince the squirrel to go chatter in another maple tree.

Chapter 2

🌷🌷🌷

"I got it!" Fawn shouted. She flew up to meet the acorn that arced through the air. "I got it!"

"Hurry, Tink!" Rani cried. Tinker Bell raced to tag a knot in a tall oak tree. Once she'd touched the knot, she zipped toward the branch above it. If she could circle the branch twice before Fawn caught the acorn, her team would get a point. If Fawn missed the acorn, Tink's team would get three points.

"I got it!" Fawn shouted again.

"You can do it, Fawn!" Rani yelled.

"Rani, who are you rooting for?" Fira called down to her friend. Rani shrugged and leaned back against a root.

"Everyone!" she said. Rani was the only fairy in Pixie Hollow who didn't have wings. Brother Dove flew her wherever she needed to go, or else she walked. She never played acorn ball. It was too difficult without her own wings. But she loved to watch.

Above, the acorn flew just beyond Fawn's grasp. Grunting, she flapped her wings with a final effort—

"Look out!" Rani cried. But nothing could stop Fawn . . . or Rosetta. They crashed right into each other. Shooting past Fawn's hand, the acorn dropped to the ground. Tinker Bell rounded the branch for the second time. The fairies on Tink's team cheered.

"Rosetta?" Fawn rubbed her side. "Did you come to join our game?"

"No, no!" Rosetta shook her head. "I need your help. There's a squirrel who is driving me crazy! Can you come get rid of him?"

"What?" Fawn asked. "You interrupted our game to ask me to get rid of a squirrel?"

"I thought you said you wanted to help me!" Rosetta wailed. "This squirrel is acting really weird." *And he's really annoying*, she added silently.

"*Hmm.*" Fawn thought for a moment.

"Maybe something is wrong. Okay, Rosetta, I'll go and talk to the squirrel." She flew off toward Rosetta's garden.

"Hey, Fawn! Where are you going?" Tinker Bell called.

"Rosetta's got a squirrel problem!" Fawn shouted over her shoulder. "I'll be back soon!"

"A squirrel problem?" Rani repeated. "I'll come with you." Getting to her feet, she whistled for Brother Dove. In a heartbeat, the bird appeared. Rani climbed onto his back. They followed Fawn and Rosetta to see what was the matter with the squirrel.

"There he is!" Rosetta pointed at the squirrel. At the sight of the fairies, he had run out to the edge of a branch and started chattering madly at them.

"He looks upset," Fawn remarked.

The squirrel chattered again as his tail twitched from side to side.

"What?" Fawn cried. "A fire?" She chattered back in Squirrel.

Rosetta's heart froze. A fire? In the forest? It could burn down all of Pixie Hollow!

Fawn said something else. The squirrel clambered down the maple trunk and bounded through the forest. Fawn zipped after him.

"What's going on?" Rosetta asked. She flew close behind Fawn. Rani and Brother Dove were right on her heels.

"There's a fire!" Fawn said. "Rani, we'll need your help." Rani was a water-talent fairy. If anyone could help with a fire, it was she.

"Hurry, Brother Dove!" Rani whispered. The bird flew like an arrow. Soon the fairies smelled smoke. Then they saw the fire. It had started in a small bush. A nearby tree was burned black at the trunk. When Rosetta saw it, she knew what had happened. The tree had been struck by lightning. The sparks must have smoldered for a while until the brush caught fire.

Orange flames licked at the brush. Rani didn't waste any time. She darted to a nearby puddle and threw fairy dust onto it. Instantly, a jet of water sprang up. Rani directed it toward the flames.

Rosetta coughed and waved her hand in front of her face. She hated the smell of smoke.

Water hissed as Rani's jet touched the flames, but it wasn't enough to stop the fire. "It's sending up sparks!" Rani cried. "The fire could spread!"

"Rosetta, gather some dew moss!" Fawn shouted. "You can throw it on the fire! I'll be back!"

Rosetta hesitated. She really didn't want to gather dew moss. It was dirty, for one thing. Plus it would stain her hands green. *Maybe if I wait just another moment, Rani will put out the fire*, Rosetta thought. *Then they won't need me to gather moss.*

Brother Dove swooped toward the flames, and Rani sent up another glittering jet of water. The fire was still burning.

She really needs my help, Rosetta thought. She was just about to fly off to find some moss when she heard a whoop.

"Ya-hoo!" Fawn hooted. The animal-talent fairy bounded toward the fire on the back of a brown rabbit. Eight more rabbits hopped behind them. The rabbits leaped into the smoke and used their enormous feet to crush the orange embers that had flown up from the bush. Rani raised her arms again. One, two, three, four, *five* jets of water blasted the flames. With a final hiss, the last flicker died out. A cottontail stamped on it, just to be sure.

"We did it!" Fawn cried happily. "Is everyone okay?"

Rani looked at Brother Dove's wing. "His feathers are a little scorched, but he's all right," she said. "We're fine."

"So is Pixie Hollow, thanks to you!" Fawn pulled Rani into a tight hug. "And to this squirrel!" She patted the animal on the shoulder and said something to him in Squirrel. Next she thanked the rabbits, who then began to hop away.

"Oh, Fawn, can you tell them not to trample my flowers?" Rosetta asked. "Since they're all here?"

Fawn and Rani turned to face Rosetta.

Neither one of them was smiling. "What happened to the dew moss?" Fawn asked.

Rosetta blushed rose pink. "Well, I—I couldn't find any." *Because I didn't look*, she added to herself.

"*Hmm,*" Fawn said.

"*Hmm,*" Rani said, too.

"Besides, it looked like you had the fire under control," Rosetta said.

"Well, the rabbits are gone," Fawn pointed out. "Maybe I'll mention it to them later."

Fawn didn't sound like she really wanted to mention it. Rosetta sighed.

That is so like Fawn. She doesn't even care about my flowers. Some fairies are just so selfish!

Chapter 3

Rosetta yawned and opened one eye. Light streamed in through the lace curtains over her bedroom window. She folded down her blanket and sat up in bed. At the window, a black-and-white butterfly caught Rosetta's eye. Its wings opened and closed slowly, as if it was waiting for her to notice it. Rosetta looked more closely. The butterfly was made out of birch bark!

"Oh my goodness!" Rosetta cried.

She hurried to the window. "It's a message from Queen Clarion!"

Rosetta held out her hand. The birch bark–paper butterfly landed lightly on her fingers and unfolded itself into a formal invitation. Rosetta read it eagerly.

Calling all fairies and sparrow men: Queen Clarion requests your presence at a dinner to honor those who saved Pixie Hollow from a forest fire.

We will meet in Buttercup Canyon.

"Dinner with the queen!" Rosetta cried. "Tonight! What in Never Land will I wear?"

Thumpthumpthump! Someone was pounding on Rosetta's door.

"It's me!" Fawn cried. She flung open the door and flew inside, waving the invitation under Rosetta's nose. "Did you see this?" she demanded.

"Yes! Isn't it wonderful?" Rosetta smiled happily.

"How can you say it's wonderful?" Fawn shrieked. "We're going to have to get dressed up!"

"Well, of course," Rosetta replied.

"But I don't want to get dressed up," Fawn complained. "I don't want to go to a special dinner!"

"Don't be ridiculous," Rosetta said. She pulled a porcupine-quill comb through her tangled hair. "It's dinner with the queen!"

"Exactly!" Fawn griped. "Dinner with lots of extra forks. Who wants that? I'd rather brush the skunks!"

"You don't mean that," Rosetta said.

"Sure I do!" Fawn fluttered toward the ceiling. "Why does the queen have to throw a fancy dinner? Why can't we just play a fun game of pea shoot?"

"Because pea shoot isn't fun," Rosetta replied.

"It's a lot more fun than getting dressed up," Fawn said.

"How would you even know whether getting dressed up is fun?" Rosetta asked. "You've never done it!"

Fawn folded her arms across her chest. "Well, how would you know that pea shoot isn't fun?" she replied. "I've never seen you try it."

"Well, I—well—" Rosetta sputtered, then stopped herself. Fawn had a point. She had never played pea shoot.

But she had watched the fairies lobbing peas at each other. It didn't look like something she would enjoy. The two fairies stared at each other for a moment.

"All right, Fawn," Rosetta said at last. "I'll make a deal with you. First you come to Queen Clarion's special dinner tonight." Fawn groaned and landed on Rosetta's bed with a plop.

"I'll help you pick out something to wear," Rosetta promised.

"What kind of a deal is that?" Fawn demanded.

"I'm not finished. Then tomorrow, I'll do anything you'd like to do," said Rosetta. "Play pea shoot or acorn ball, or whatever."

Fawn let out a whoop. "Then you'll see that pea shoot is way more fun than going to a fancy dinner!" She flipped in midair.

"No," Rosetta said, shaking her head. "*You'll* see how much fun it is to put on a beautiful outfit and eat a fancy dinner. We'll need to go to the sewing talents and choose something to wear, but first I need some time to get dressed and fix my hair. Come back in an hour."

Fawn looked doubtful.

"Okay, an hour and a half," Rosetta said. "But don't be late! We'll need as much time as possible to get ready!"

Chapter 4

"I love it!" Rosetta cried.

The sewing-talent fairies had just pulled a beautiful dress made of violets over her head. "Plus it's a perfect fit!" Rosetta added. "Fawn!" she called. "Are you having any luck with that dress?"

Fawn pulled aside the green-and-white leaf that served as a dressing room curtain and flew into the center of the room. She was wearing a lacy white dress made of dandelion fluff.

"You look gorgeous!" Rosetta smiled happily at Fawn.

Fawn scratched at her waist. "It's itchy," she complained.

"Oh, Fawn!" Rosetta shook her head. "First the rose-petal dress was too poufy. Then the poppy dress was too long and got caught in your wings!" She gave an exasperated sigh.

Fawn shrugged. "I just want to be comfortable."

"Fancy dresses aren't comfortable," Rosetta shot back. "They're beautiful. And look at yourself." Taking her friend by the hand, Rosetta led her to the mirror. "You have to admit that you look amazing."

Fawn blinked in surprise at her reflection. "It *is* very pretty," she admitted.

"That's it." Rosetta nodded in approval. "That's the dress. So stop scratching."

"But it itches!" Fawn said again.

"You'll get used to it." Rosetta shrugged. "Are you ready to go to the shoemaking talent?"

"Rosetta, my wings are tired!" Fawn moaned. "We've already picked out jewelry, perfume, and stockings!"

"And we still have to go to the hairdressing talent, too! Oh, come on." Rosetta put her hands on her hips. "I don't understand you, Fawn. You can spend all day trooping through the forest and not get tired!"

"But that's different."

"It sure is," Rosetta agreed. "You don't get muddy and dirty trying on perfume!" She turned to the sewing-talent fairies. "We'll take these dresses!"

"We'll see you at dinner!" Thimble called as Rosetta and Fawn flew out the door.

An hour later, Rosetta was satisfied. They had everything they needed for the dinner. "I can't believe I got a pair of pink shoes," Fawn said. She was carrying three huge leaf bags and a shoe box.

"They were the most beautiful shoes there," Rosetta insisted.

Fawn sighed. Just then, a large golden dragonfly darted past them. It was flying so fast that Rosetta felt the breeze from its wings against her face.

With a whoop, Fawn dropped her bags and her box and took off after the golden insect.

"Fawn!" Rosetta screeched. But Fawn wasn't listening.

Then Rosetta noticed the leaf bags fluttering toward the ground, right toward a puddle. "Not the shoes!" she cried.

With a burst of speed, she swooped in to catch the rose-petal slippers. "Gotcha!" Rosetta collected the bags as they floated past her.

Fawn and the dragonfly wound around a white birch tree in a spiral. Rosetta watched as they raced. "I'd better stop her before she makes a mess of herself," Rosetta said. She zipped toward the blue pansies.

"Fawn!" Rosetta yelled. She dropped between her friend and the pansies and held out both hands.

Fawn stopped short. Rosetta was loaded down with bags and Fawn's box. Her face was stormy.

"Rosetta!" Fawn squeaked. "See you some other time, Flitterwing," Fawn told the dragonfly. It buzzed away.

Rosetta thrust the bags at her friend. "You dropped these," she said.

"Oops." Sheepishly, Fawn took the bags.

Rosetta's anger faded. She knew that her friend couldn't help getting excited when a dragonfly wanted to race. But still—it was too silly. "You can't just go dragonfly racing when we have things to do," Rosetta scolded.

"You're right," Fawn admitted. "I didn't mean to."

"It's okay," Rosetta told her. "But let's hurry. We still have to get our hair done and get dressed before dinner." She started off toward the Home Tree. Would Fawn ever get the hang of having Rosetta's kind of fun?

Chapter 5

🌷🌷🌷

Pink and gold clouds hovered over Buttercup Canyon. Thousands of tiny pink and yellow flowers carpeted the valley. At the edge of the canyon, dozens upon dozens of fireflies glowed over crisp white tablecloths set with plates of gleaming mother-of-pearl. The tables were beginning to fill up with fairies.

"Oh, look," Rosetta said with a gasp. "There's Fira! Her cardinal-feather dress is gorgeous! Rani and Tink are with her. I just love what Tink's done with her hair!"

Fawn trailed behind her friend. "I'm itchy," she said.

"Oh, stop complaining," Rosetta told her. Waving her hands, she called, "Fira! Tink! Rani! Over here!"

"Brass buckles, Fawn!" Tink cried, flying right past Rosetta. "You look so beautiful!"

"Is that dress made of dandelion fluff?" Fira gushed.

Rani gave Fawn an enormous smile. "It looks great on you."

Fawn's glow—already ruddy in the light from the setting sun—turned even pinker. "Rosetta helped me pick it out," she said.

Rosetta beamed.

"Wow, Rosetta," Tink said, "Fawn looks great!"

Clearing her throat, Rosetta struck a pose. *And now,* she thought, *it's time for someone to notice my dress!*

But everyone was so busy fluttering around Fawn that no one noticed her lovely dress. Or her darling little slippers. Just then, Grace, one of the queen's helpers, flew over. In a formal voice, she said, "Queen Clarion would like to invite you to sit at her table."

Rosetta's heart pattered double-time. Sit with the queen! What an honor!

"That's nice, but we're already sitting with our friends," Fawn said.

Rosetta gaped in surprise. "You just insulted the queen!" she cried.

"She doesn't look insulted," Tink said.

Rosetta saw that Queen Clarion herself was flying over. A delicate crown sparkled in the queen's golden hair, and she wore a lovely yellow ruffled daffodil dress. Whenever Rosetta saw the queen, she became terribly nervous.

"Fawn, I understand that you want to eat dinner with your friends," the queen said in her gentle voice. "I hope you don't mind if I join you."

"We'd be honored!" Rosetta cried. She pulled out the chair beside hers.

Queen Clarion settled between Rosetta and Fawn. Rani sat at the end of the table with Brother Dove nestled beside her.

I'm sitting next to Queen Clarion! Rosetta thought giddily. She searched her mind for something clever to say. But she couldn't think of a single thing.

"Fawn, your dress is lovely," Queen Clarion said.

"It's very itchy," Fawn said.

Rosetta couldn't believe her friend had said such a thing to the queen!

But Queen Clarion just laughed her sparkly laugh. "My shoes are too tight," she admitted.

A serving talent flew over. She was carrying an enormous soup tureen. With a smile, she ladled some squash-blossom soup into Fawn's bowl.

Please don't slurp, Rosetta begged silently. Fawn *did* slurp. Rosetta bit her lip and forced herself not to say anything. She hoped the queen noticed that she wasn't slurping.

After a while, the queen stood up. "Attention, everyone," she called, tapping her glass. A hush fell over the fairies. They turned to look at their queen.

"We're gathered here tonight to honor

certain fairies," Queen Clarion announced. "As you all know, there was a fire at the edge of the forest. It could have burned all of Pixie Hollow, if it weren't for some very brave fairies."

Rosetta sat up in her chair.

"First, there was the fairy who used her water talent to fight the flames," the queen said. "Step forward, Rani."

The queen hung a silver necklace around Rani's neck. Rani smiled. Her blue eyes brimmed with happy tears. "Rani could not have put out the fire without help," the queen went on. "Brother Dove flew close to the flames to make sure the job got done."

Queen Clarion hung a silver necklace around his neck. "And we are grateful to Fawn," the queen said. "She realized that there was a fire and brought a herd of rabbits to stamp out the sparks."

Fawn bowed her head so that the queen could slide a silver necklace over it. The cheers echoed through Buttercup Canyon.

Rosetta clapped with the others. Then she turned to Queen Clarion, her face tilted up, her eyes dancing. She knew what was coming next.

"I'm glad you all could come to this very special dinner," Queen Clarion said. "It's truly wonderful to honor these fairies for their good deeds."

Rosetta sat at the table, stunned. She was still waiting for the queen to mention her name. After all, she was the one who'd flown to get Fawn. And she would have helped put out the fire if she could have done something besides collect dew moss. Surely she should get some credit for trying—shouldn't she?

But the queen had already flown off. The ceremony was over.

"Isn't it pretty?" Fawn asked. She held the silver necklace up to the moonlight.

"Beautiful!" Fira said.

"I can't believe she gave one to each of us!" Rani said.

"Rosetta, you were right!" Fawn cried. "This really was a fun night!"

Rosetta hadn't thought it was very fun at all. Nobody had noticed her dress. The queen had barely spoken to her. And she was the only one who had been at the fire who hadn't gotten a silver necklace! She wanted to be happy for Fawn. She wanted to be, but she wasn't.

Chapter 6

"Wake up, sleepyhead!" Fawn sang as she flew into Rosetta's room. "It's time to have some fun!"

Groaning, Rosetta buried her head under her fluffy pillow.

Fawn reached down and yanked the pillow off Rosetta's head. "Don't tell me that you're going to back out on your promise, Rosetta."

"I never go back on my promises,"

Rosetta mumbled. "But don't you think we should wait until tomorrow?" Rosetta didn't want to get out from under her comfortable blankets just to play acorn ball or race dragonflies, or whatever it was that Fawn had in mind. "I'm a little tired from the party last night—"

Fawn laughed. "You won't feel tired once you see what I've got planned!"

Rosetta cleared her throat. "We're not going to do anything"—she searched for the right word—"gross...are we?"

Fawn laughed. "Of course not! Now, hurry and get dressed. We don't want to waste the whole day!"

Rosetta sighed. It was clear that Fawn wasn't going to give her any hints about her plans for the day. Rosetta pulled on a fresh rose-petal skirt and blouse but stopped before putting on her shoes. Should she wear her new pair—the ones made of delicate violet petals? *Well, Fawn said we won't be doing anything gross*, Rosetta thought. She slipped her toes into the shoes. Then she brushed her hair, straightened her wings, and tidied her bed. "All right," she said at last, "I'm ready. Where are we off to?"

"Not so fast," Fawn said. "First you have to put on this blindfold." She held out a scarf made from a tender blade of grass.

Rosetta frowned at the scarf. "How can I fly wearing a blindfold?" she asked. "I'll run into a tree!"

"Don't worry. I'll lead you." Fawn tied the scarf over Rosetta's eyes. "Can you see?" she asked.

"Nothing but darkness," Rosetta replied.

"Perfect!" Fawn giggled. Tugging on Rosetta's hand, she pulled her through the Home Tree and out into the center of Pixie Hollow. Fawn was very careful to watch out for Rosetta.

Rosetta realized that her other senses were keener with the blindfold on. She noticed the feel of the warm sun on her wings, and then she was struck by the sweet smell of flowers. "Are we going to my garden for a game of butterfly tag?" she asked.

"We won't be too far away from your garden," Fawn answered playfully, pulling Rosetta along, "but that's not where we're going."

After a while, Rosetta heard the bubbling of rushing water. "Are we going to spend the day at Havendish Stream?"

"You've guessed it!" Fawn cried. She led Rosetta to a seat on the bank.

"Oh, what fun!" Rosetta clapped her hands. She pictured herself floating along on a leaf boat, enjoying the sun as Fawn pointed out the pretty fish that swam below. "Fawn, you're brilliant! You're absolutely—" Rosetta's words stuck in her throat when Fawn pulled away her blindfold.

Sitting in the water at the bank of the stream were two enormous green bull-frogs. Both were wearing harnesses made of bark rope.

"*Ribbit!*" one of them said.

"We're going frog-riding!" Fawn said with a whoop.

"I thought you said we weren't going to do anything gross!" Rosetta wailed.

"What's gross about frogs?" Fawn asked.

One of the frogs seemed to agree. "*Ribbit!*"

Rosetta stared at her friend. Fawn was completely serious. She believed that frog-riding was a fun, non-gross activity. Fawn's eyes were shining, and her cheeks were pink with excitement. *I can't refuse to go,* Rosetta thought. *I promised I'd do whatever she wanted. Me and my big mouth.*

Chapter 7

Fawn splashed through the ankle-deep water toward the bullfrogs. Rosetta waited on the bank. "I've never been frog-riding," she said.

"It's easy!" Fawn held out the reins attached to the harness on the smaller frog. "I'll show you."

Rosetta didn't want to ruin her new shoes, so she fluttered toward the frog.

"Just drop into the saddle." Fawn gestured toward the almond shell on the frog's back.

Rosetta hovered for a moment, unsure. "Where do I put my feet?"

"On the frog," Fawn said.

Rosetta grimaced. *I don't want my new shoes to touch that slimy frog*, she thought. But she didn't want to say that to Fawn. "All right," she said at last. She dropped daintily into the almond shell.

"See?" Fawn grinned at her friend. "Nothing to be afraid of!"

The frog shifted beneath Rosetta. *"Eek!"* she cried. She windmilled her arms, then leaned forward and grabbed the frog's neck. His skin was cool and damp.

Looking down, Rosetta found herself staring into a giant yellow eye. "Yikes!" she shouted.

"You're scaring Strongjump," Fawn said. She croaked at him in Frog. "I told him to calm down," she explained. "You're not going to hurt him."

Rosetta couldn't believe the frog could be afraid of *her*!

"If you want Strongjump to go right, pull the reins to the right," Fawn explained. "If you want to go left, pull the reins left."

"And what if I want to stop and get off?" Rosetta muttered.

"Then pull the reins toward you," Fawn told her. "And if you want him to go faster, just give him a little poke—like this!" She reached out and touched Strongjump's side.

"*Ribbit!*" Strongjump took a giant leap forward.

He landed with a plop and a splash on a

nearby lily pad. Rosetta grabbed the reins more tightly.

"Come on, Swiftlegs!" Fawn called to her frog. "Let's go!"

Swiftlegs hopped along the edge of Havendish Stream. He sent up a spray of water around him. Strongjump leaped after Swiftlegs. Rosetta felt as if she were trying to fly in a windstorm.

"Just hang on!" Fawn shouted. Swiftlegs led the way from stone to stone, then across the stream on lily pads. "Plant your feet. That will keep you steady!"

Rosetta jammed her feet against Strongjump's sides and clung to the reins. She squeezed her eyes shut. "Tell me when it's over!"

Fawn laughed. "You're a natural frogrider!"

"I am?" Rosetta opened one eye wide enough to see a gold-and-black bumblebee buzz into a bright purple water lily. Silver moss hung like a lacy curtain from tree branches that reached like fingers across the stream. Rosetta caught her breath. For a garden fairy, this was a water paradise. She'd flown beside Havendish Stream more times than she could count, but she'd never seen it from a frog's-eye view before. "It's beautiful!" she yelled over to Fawn. Fawn pulled Swiftlegs's reins to the left, and she and the frog splashed through the shallow water.

Rosetta yanked on Strongjump's reins. She must not have done it the right way, because the bullfrog stopped short. Rosetta's right foot slipped off his shoulder, and she tumbled into the air.

"Rosetta, what are you doing?" Fawn called, pulling Swiftlegs to a stop.

"Falling!" Rosetta cried. One violet-petal shoe flew off. It arced toward the edge of the stream. "My shoe!" she shrieked. Beating her wings, Rosetta righted herself and dove after the shoe. She reached out—

Splash!

"Hey," Fawn said from the back of her bullfrog. "Good job—you got it."

Rosetta's hand was raised over her head. In it she held a dry violet-petal shoe. Unfortunately, though, the rest of her—including her *other* shoe—had landed in Havendish Stream. Her wings felt heavy on her back. They were too wet for her to fly.

Fawn hopped off Swiftlegs's back. She helped Rosetta stand up. Mud squished ickily through the toes of Rosetta's bare foot. "Are you okay?" Fawn asked.

Rosetta took a deep breath. *This isn't Fawn's fault*, she thought. *I said I would do whatever she wanted for a whole day.* "I'm fine," she said.

"I don't think we should do any more frog-riding. Not until you dry out." Fawn eyed Rosetta's soggy wings. "But don't worry! Our fun day isn't over!"

Rosetta gulped.

"Maybe we should go strawberry picking," Fawn suggested. "That's something we can do without flying."

Strawberries? That didn't sound so bad. In fact, Rosetta loved sweets. "Should we go to my garden?" she suggested. "I've got lots of strawberries."

"Wild berries taste better," Fawn said.

"I don't know about that," Rosetta huffed.

"*Ribbit?*" Swiftlegs said. Next to him, Strongjump was sunning himself on a lily pad.

"We've finished," Fawn told them in Frog language. "See you soon!"

Chapter 8

"Where did you say you saw those strawberries, again?" Rosetta asked.

Fawn fluttered ahead and then darted back. "Not much farther!"

Rosetta kept her eyes glued to Fawn. She didn't want to lose sight of her friend. After all, the farther into the forest they went, the darker it got. Fawn was used to having adventures in the woods, but Rosetta wasn't. It wouldn't be fun to get lost!

Rip!

"Oh, hazelnuts!" Rosetta cried. A piece of her red skirt was caught on the tiny fierce thorns of a prickleberry bush. Carefully, Rosetta pulled the piece of petal from the bush. She wasn't sure whether the sewing-talent fairies could fix her skirt, but it was worth asking them. She put the piece into her pocket.

"There they are!" Fawn shouted.

Looking up, Rosetta realized that she could no longer see her friend. "Fawn!" she cried. "Where are you?"

"Follow my voice!" Fawn called.

Rosetta shook her wings, but they still weren't completely dry. She would have to continue walking. As she took another step, her dainty shoe stuck in the mud, and her toes slipped right out of it. "Oh, no—

my one good shoe!" she said. She hopped backward to try to pick up the shoe, but her heavy wings threw her off balance. Rosetta flailed her arms.

Plop!

She fell face-first into the mud puddle.

"Rosetta!" Fawn cried, flying into view just overhead. "Are you all right?"

Rosetta gritted her teeth. "I'm fine." She grabbed her shoe. It was, of course, covered in mud. Just like the front of her dress.

She slipped her muddy shoe onto her foot. It squished as she walked. *At least it matches the one that got wet in the river*, she thought.

"Oh." Fawn nodded. "Well, okay. The berries are right over here! Isn't this great?" With a whoop, Fawn fluttered ahead.

Rosetta took a deep breath. *I'm dirty,*

she thought, *my wings are wet, and my skirt is torn. And Fawn doesn't even seem to care. Why should she? She's dry. Her clothes aren't torn. She doesn't have a speck of mud on her.*

Finally, Rosetta caught up to Fawn, who was pointing to a green leaf the size of a fairy umbrella. Below it was a plump, red wild strawberry speckled with seeds.

"Look!" Fawn exclaimed. "We can each carry one back to Dulcie! She can probably make ten pies with these."

Rosetta's mouth watered at the thought. Maybe the day wouldn't turn out to be so horrible after all.

"I have an idea," Fawn said suddenly. "Let's split one!" She picked a strawberry and held it out to Rosetta. "You first."

Rosetta smiled and took a bite. She felt

better after a single mouthful. She handed the strawberry back to Fawn and sat down on a toadstool.

"It's nice to be in the sunshine," Rosetta said. She tested her wings. They were finally dry.

"It sure is," Fawn agreed. She sat down next to Rosetta. "See? Isn't this a terrific day?" she asked.

Rosetta was about to say yes. But at that moment, a spider dropped right in front of her face. Rosetta flew two feet in the air, screeching. "*Eek!* Get it away from me!"

Fawn started laughing so hard that she fell off her toadstool.

"Help!" Rosetta shrieked.

"It's just a baby spider," called Fawn.

"That's easy for you to say!" Rosetta shouted back. "It didn't attack you!"

Fawn flew over to her friend and put a hand on her shoulder. "Rosetta, it's okay," she said.

Whimpering, Rosetta hovered as Fawn caught the small gray spider. She placed it on the trunk of the golden tree. "Go on," Fawn told the spider. "Go back to your web."

The little spider skittered up the tree. But when Fawn turned to face her friend, she saw that Rosetta wasn't smiling.

"What's wrong?" Fawn asked.

"This has been the worst day ever!" Rosetta griped. "I got all wet. I fell in the mud. I ruined my dress. Then a creepy, crawly spider attacked me—and you just laughed!"

"But—but—we're having fun," Fawn sputtered.

"No, we aren't!" Rosetta cried. "Maybe you're having fun, but I'm having a horrible time! I want to go home!"

Fawn looked surprised. For a moment, she didn't speak.

Tears sparkled in Rosetta's eyes.

"Okay, Rosetta," Fawn said at last. "Let's go home."

Chapter 9

🌷🌷🌷

"Oh, look, Rosetta!" Fawn dove toward a tree with red leaves. A vine with small silver flowers climbed up the trunk. "Angel blooms!"

Rosetta usually loved seeing beautiful flowers. Plus, angel blooms were very rare—even in Pixie Hollow. But Rosetta barely glanced at the flowers. "That's nice," she said. She flew on toward the Home Tree.

Fawn fluttered after her. "Hey," she said

suddenly, "do you want to collect some honey? I know a hive that isn't too far from here."

Rosetta shuddered at the thought of sticky honey. She knew Fawn was trying to cheer her up. But the only things that would improve her mood were a bath, a change of clothes, and a new pair of shoes. "I'd rather just go home."

Fawn nodded slowly. "Okay."

The two flew side by side in silence for a while. They were almost at the edge of the forest when they heard a low coo, then another. The sound seemed to be coming from a nearby tree.

"What's that?" Fawn asked.

Rosetta pretended not to hear her. *"Coo, coo."* Peeking into a hole in the wood, Fawn saw three huge pairs of eyes. They were surrounded by soft, dark feathers. Three baby owls blinked up at her.

"Oh, how lovely!" Fawn cried. All fairies—even animal-talent fairies—were afraid of grown owls. But these babies were adorable! "Rosetta!" she called. "You have to see this!"

"What now?" Rosetta muttered.

"You three stay right there," Fawn told the babies, who cooed at her. "Rosetta! Rosetta!" she called. Quick as a flash, she darted after her friend. But she was distracted by the owls. She ran into a tree branch.

"*Oof!*" Fawn dropped to the ground… right into a mole hole! Rosetta turned. But she hadn't seen what had happened to Fawn. As far as she knew, Fawn had just vanished.

"Where did that fairy go?" she mumbled.

"Fawn?" she called, but she still didn't see her friend. "Fawn?"

"Down here!" cried Fawn.

Rosetta flew toward the ground. "Where are you?"

"I'm under your feet!" Fawn called.

Looking down, Rosetta noticed a large hole. She peeked inside. Fawn was in there. Her face was streaked with dirt. "Are you all right?" Rosetta asked.

"I'm not hurt," Fawn said. "But my wings are trapped. Can you help me out?" She stretched out a hand, but she was still more than a fairy arm's length from the edge of the hole.

Rosetta was about to reach for her friend's hand when a big ugly black beetle scrambled out of the hole. Then she noticed that there were worms—creepy, crawly, slimy worms—oozing out of the dirt over Fawn's head.

Rosetta jumped to her feet and grimaced. "I can't," she said.

"You can't?" Fawn sounded confused. "Why not?"

Rosetta looked at the beetle and the worms. *Oooh*, they were so icky! But she didn't want to tell Fawn the truth. Fawn probably thought that worms and beetles weren't gross at all.

She'll just tell me not to be afraid, like she did with the spider, Rosetta thought. *Or she'll laugh again*. "I—I can't reach you," Rosetta said.

"You can if you lean into the hole a little," Fawn said.

Rosetta shook her head.

Fawn looked at her friend for a moment. "Is it because of the worms?" she asked.

Rosetta wanted to say *No, no, of course not.* But she just couldn't lie to Fawn. "Yes!" she wailed, bursting into tears.

"It's okay, Rosetta," Fawn said. "I understand."

Rosetta was so surprised that she stopped crying. "You do?"

"Sure I do," Fawn said. "We're friends, aren't we? Don't worry, Rosetta. I'm not afraid of worms. I'll be fine here in the hole for a while. Why don't you just go get one of the other animal-talent fairies to come help me?"

Rosetta heaved a huge sigh of relief. "Great idea!" she said. "I'll fly like the wind!"

"I'll be waiting," Fawn said.

Rosetta scrambled to her feet and shot into the air—then she stopped.

Wait a minute, Rosetta thought. *What am I doing? Fawn is my friend! I can't just leave her alone in a dark, wormy hole. Can I?* Rosetta dropped back to the ground and kneeled at the edge. "Shoo!" she said, waving at the beetle. Once it had waddled off, she stuck her face near the hole. "Okay, Fawn. I'm going to help you out!"

"You don't have to do this," Fawn called. "You can just fly for help, like you did with the squirrel."

"That was different," Rosetta told her. "I'm not an animal talent. I couldn't even talk to him! Besides, you're not a squirrel. You're my friend."

Taking a deep breath, Rosetta stuck her

hand into the hole. She whimpered as her fingers touched a slimy worm. It wriggled under her hand, and Rosetta's whimper turned into a moan. *Don't think about it,* she told herself. Slowly, she forced her hand deeper into the hole. *Don't think about how gross it is!* Now she could feel worms all along the length of her arm. *Ooh, but it's so gross,* she thought.

"Almost there!" Fawn called. Rosetta closed her hand on something that felt like Fawn's hand—until it squirmed. Rosetta's neck went cold. She wanted to run away. Instead, she forced herself to reach farther.

"Got it!" Fawn cried.

Rosetta felt Fawn's strong hand in hers.

"Now pull!" Fawn called.

Rosetta strained her wings and used both arms to try to drag Fawn out of the hole. Nothing happened. Rosetta pulled harder. She flapped with all her might. Finally, Fawn broke free. She popped out of the hole so suddenly that both fairies tumbled backward. They landed in a bed of soft moss. Fawn propped herself up on her arms and looked at her friend. "Are you okay?"

Rosetta blinked twice. "I think so," she said. Then she started to giggle. "I saved you from the worms!"

Fawn laughed, too. "You did! I can't believe it, but you did."

Rosetta sat up and put her arm around Fawn's shoulders. "That's what friends are for," she said.

Chapter 10

"Ahh," Rosetta said. She stepped into a fresh rose-petal dress. "That's better." She smiled at herself in the mirror.

As she slipped her foot into a dainty slipper, a birch-bark butterfly flew up to her window. She held out her hand. The butterfly landed, unfolding into a card.

Rosetta read the invitation. "Queen Clarion wants to see me right away?" she cried. "But I don't even have time to put on a fancy gown!" She groaned and fluttered out of her room.

When Rosetta got to the queen's quarters, Fawn was already there.

"Ah, Rosetta," Queen Clarion said, "come have a cup of tea with us."

Rosetta felt a stab of envy. Fawn was having tea with the queen? Still, Rosetta made her way over to the table. It was set with white linens of the finest spider silk. Plates were heaped with poppy puff rolls, tiny cucumber-seed sandwiches, and sweet honey cakes.

"Have one of these," Fawn said. She held out a plate of small strawberry tarts. "They're made with the wild strawberry we picked today!"

"They are?" Rosetta bit into the crumbly

tart. It was even more delicious than she had imagined it would be.

"Fawn has been telling me the most exciting story," Queen Clarion said. She paused to take a sip of her tea.

"Really?" Rosetta hoped she wouldn't have to sit and listen to another story about Fawn riding a turtle or a groundhog or a bat.

"She tells me that you rescued her," the queen said. Her lips curved into a smile.

"What?" Rosetta's teacup clattered against her saucer. "No, no—she fell into a hole and I helped her out, that's all."

"She made it sound much more dangerous than that," the queen said.

"It was a very deep hole," Fawn said quickly. "And it was full of worms."

"That must have been very frightening," Queen Clarion said to Rosetta.

"Well, it was," Rosetta admitted. "But most fairies wouldn't have been afraid of a few worms."

"The question is not what other fairies would be afraid of," the queen said reasonably. "The question is what you were afraid of, and how brave you managed to be for your friend."

Rosetta was quiet. She looked down at her hands. How could she have been brave when she had been terribly scared the whole time?

"Therefore, because you were so brave, I would like to give you this." Queen Clarion reached into a blue silk bag and pulled out a silver necklace. It was just like the one Fawn wore around her neck.

"It's beautiful," Rosetta said as the queen held it up.

"You've earned it, Rosetta," the queen said. She placed her teacup on the table and fluttered over to help Rosetta with the clasp. "There's something else I'd like to show you." Queen Clarion beckoned Rosetta to the window.

Rosetta gasped at what she saw. Fairies—hundreds of them—were gathered below. When they saw Rosetta, they cheered.

"We didn't have time to prepare dinner in Buttercup Canyon," the queen explained. "But I've asked the cooking-talent fairies to serve dinner in the courtyard. And you'll be the guest of honor, Rosetta."

Rosetta looked at Fawn, who smiled a little sheepishly. "I wanted to make sure that your special dinner happened today, before sundown," Fawn said. "I know our adventure wasn't very much fun for you. I thought dinner would make up for it."

"Why?" Rosetta asked.

"Well, I wanted you to have as much fun today as I had yesterday," Fawn said.

"But I didn't do anything as brave as what you did," Rosetta told her friend.

"That isn't true. What you did was very brave," Fawn said. "Everyone has different fears."

"You're not afraid of anything," Rosetta pointed out.

"Sure I am! I'm afraid of dandelion dresses and perfume and fancy dinners," Fawn said. She squeezed Rosetta's hand. "I'm afraid of tearing spider-silk stockings and of having my braid fall into the soup. That dinner was terrifying!"

Rosetta thought about that. For Fawn, putting out the fire had been easy...as easy as slipping into a new dress was for Rosetta. It was strange to think that they could be so different and still be such good friends.

"Don't worry, Fawn," Rosetta said. "I'll always help you with dresses and dinners and things like that."

"Shall we go to dinner?" Queen Clarion suggested.

Rosetta and Fawn followed Queen Clarion to the courtyard. How things had changed in a few hours! It had been a truly horrible day. Rosetta thought about her ruined shoes, her muddy dress, the scary spider, and the creepy worms. But there had been some lovely parts, too. She'd never forget how pretty Havendish Stream looked from the back of a frog. Or how wonderful a wild strawberry tasted when you picked it yourself.

She fingered the silver necklace around her neck. Could the worst day of a fairy's life also be the best? *I never knew that a horrible day could become so nice*, she thought. *But it just did.*